To Clare Hair

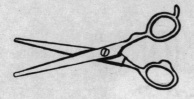

JACK
BEECHWHISTLE

RISE of the
HAIRY HORROR

by **Kes Gray**

RED FOX

RED FOX

UK | USA | Canada | Ireland | Australia
India | New Zealand | South Africa

Red Fox is part of the Penguin Random House group of companies
whose addresses can be found at global.penguinrandomhouse.com.

www.penguin.co.uk   www.puffin.co.uk   www.ladybird.co.uk

Penguin
Random House
UK

First published 2017

001

Text and character copyright © Kes Gray, 2017
Cover illustration copyright © Nick Sharratt, 2017
Inside illustrations copyright © Garry Parsons, 2017

The moral right of the author and illustrators has been asserted

Set in VAG Rounded 15/23pt
Printed in Great Britain by Clays Ltd, St Ives plc

A CIP catalogue record for this book is available from the British Library

ISBN: 978–1–782–95304–3

All correspondence to:
Red Fox
Penguin Random House Children's
80 Strand, London WC2R 0RL

CHAPTER 1

Hi, Jack "Dragon" Beechwhistle here, Junior Defender of the World. Have you heard that daddy-longlegs are full of the most dangerous poison known to man, which means if they had teeth they would be the most dangerous insects on the planet? Well, that's what my best friends Harry and Colin are saying.

Actually it's not true. Daddy-long-legs don't have any poison in them

1

at all. I've just checked it out on a website that has real scientists giving you real answers on it. That's one of the ways I've become an expert in so many things: by listening to experts.

Knowing your facts is really important if you are going to become a world defence agent. Facts are the things that help you decide how dangerous a mission is going to be.

For instance, if you were on a jungle mission and you were going to land your super-fast jet on a really small island, you would need to know your facts, like how long the runway is. If you were landing on a really small island and you hadn't found out how long the runway was, you could end up coming in too fast, running out of runway, skidding off the end, crashing into the sea and then having to wrestle sharks or sea monsters and stuff.

Or say you were on a space mission and an immense asteroid was about to collide with your spacecraft. If asteroids have a weak spot and you know exactly where the weak spot is, then you will know exactly whereabouts to aim your defence missiles. Get your facts wrong and end up aiming at a strong

spot instead of a weak spot, and it won't be the asteroid that e x p l o d e s into a million pieces. It will be you.

I don't know if asteroids actually do have a weak spot, by the way. It's one of the things I'll be looking into next. When I find out, I will add it to my Fact File under *A* for *Asteroid*.

I've been building a World Defence Fact File for about two years. I started it after my dad told me I'd been made a world defence agent just like him. Well, a junior one. My Fact File is divided up into loads of different sections, going from *A* for *Asteroid* to *Z* for *Zombies*. Each section is full of handy tips that will keep you safe. When it's finished I'm going to put it on the internet so that everyone on the planet can learn from my knowledge and be a hundred times safer in an instant.

At the moment the only people I share my knowledge with are Harry and Colin. Harry and Colin live in my street and we're in the same class at school. I'm training them to be junior world defence agents like me. Both of them have a lot to learn – like *never* get your hair cut at Valentino's.

Valentino is the hairdresser in the High Street. At least, it says he's a hairdresser on the outside of his shop. When I saw what he'd done to Harry and Colin at the end of the summer holidays, I knew it couldn't be true.

I was sitting on the wall outside my house when I finally saw them coming down the street on their bikes. At first I couldn't see what had happened to them because as they rode up to me and parked their bikes, they both had their hoods up. When they took their hoods down, I realized why.

"What kind of haircut do you call that?" I asked.

"A 'light trim'," sighed Harry.

"My mum told me to ask for a light trim too," groaned Colin.

"There is no way those are light trims," I said, getting up from the wall to see what their haircuts looked like from behind. "YOU'VE BEEN TOTALLY SCALPED!"

"It does feel a bit short," said Colin, rubbing the back of his head.

"It's a lot short," I told them.

"How long do you reckon it will take to grow back?" asked Harry, putting his hood back up and sitting

10

down on the wall.

"About two years." I smiled.

"Very funny," sighed Colin, putting his hood up too.

"Are you sure you went into a hairdresser's?" I asked. "Are you sure you didn't walk into a lawnmower shop by mistake?"

"One more joke and I'm going home," said Harry.

"Me too," grumbled Colin.

Harry and Colin were right: it was no time for jokes. I had two wounded men who needed my support.

"OK!" I said. "No more jokes, I promise."

"Swear the secret swear," said Harry.

"I swear," I said, folding my arms across my chest and then doing five blinks and a double thumbs-up.

"We've got to go back to school on Monday," said Colin, dropping his bike on the pavement and sitting beside Harry. "And we've got to walk into the playground looking like this."

"Everyone's gonna laugh their heads off," added Harry.

"I hope Daisy Butters and Gabriella Summers get their hair cut at Valentino's before we go back to school too." Colin laughed.

"Can you imagine it?!"

Daisy Butters and Gabriella Summers are the two most annoying girls in school. All of us could imagine it.

"No such luck," I sighed.

"I mean, how can you go to a hairdresser's asking for a light trim and then get totally scalped?" sighed Harry, kicking his front tyre. "It's so wrong."

"So why didn't Valentino give us what we asked him to give us?" asked Colin.

It was a good question. There are haircuts, there are bad haircuts and there are criminal haircuts. Had they just had their hair cut by a criminal?

"Maybe, just maybe," I said, "there is more to Valentino than meets the eye."

"What do you mean?"

"I don't know what I mean yet," I told them, "but I'm calling an emergency meeting NOW!

WORLD DEFENCE TIP:

If you need to have emergency meetings, make sure you have a secret den to have them in.

"Let's go!" I said, grabbing my bike and speeding off in the direction of Allotment 24. "I can feel a new mission coming on!"

CHAPTER 2

Me, Colin and Harry have the best secret den in the world. It's so secret, only we know it's there. Or at least, only we know how to get in. From the outside it looks like a padlocked shed in an overgrown allotment. But from the inside it's everything a secret den should be.

As soon as we arrived, we camouflaged our bikes, took the lid off our water butt and climbed down into our secret tunnel.

Colin was the first one in.

Then Harry.

Then me.

At 11:11 hundred hours precisely our emergency meeting began.

WORLD DEFENCE TIP:
Always carry a small pad and pen in case you need to make emergency notes. If you don't have a pad, make one out of something else.

"OK," I said, wiping the dirt off an old gardening pencil and then leaning a carrot-seed packet against my knees. "Tell me everything that happened at Valentino's."

"I got there first," said Colin.

"And I got there second," said Harry.

"Did you notice anything suspicious when you entered the shop?" I asked.

"Not really," said Colin. "There were three people already waiting in the queue though."

"Did any of the people in the queue look suspicious?" I asked.

"There was a man reading a newspaper," said Harry.

"Was the newspaper the right way up?" I asked.

WORLD DEFENCE TIP:
Beware of upside-down newspapers.
People reading upside-down
newspapers are only pretending
to read their newspapers. They are
definitely spies and have probably
got their eyes on you!

"I didn't notice," said Harry.

"Was it a foreign newspaper?"
I asked.

WORLD DEFENCE TIP:
Beware of people reading foreign
newspapers. If you see someone reading
a foreign newspaper, they could be a
foreign agent. If they are reading a
foreign newspaper upside down, they
are definitely a foreign agent.

"I didn't notice," said Harry.

"Did it have eyeholes cut out of it?" I asked.

WORLD DEFENCE TIP:

Beware of newspapers with eyeholes. If you see anyone reading a newspaper or magazine with eyeholes cut out, then they are using the eyeholes to spy on you. If you see someone reading an upside-down foreign newspaper with eyeholes, RUN!

"I didn't notice," said Harry and Colin together.

"OK," I said, drawing a cross on the back of the seed packet and trying a different approach. "What DID you notice?"

"How do you mean?" asked Colin.

"I mean, was anyone in the queue wearing suspicious clothes?" I said.

"What sort of suspicious clothes?" asked Colin.

"Black hat, black shirt, black gloves, black coat, dark glasses, army camo, Ninja robes, gas mask, bulletproof vest – anything you wouldn't normally see in a queue at the hairdresser's," I explained.

"I didn't really notice what anyone

was wearing," said Colin. "I was too busy watching Valentino."

"So was I," said Harry.

It wasn't the best start to an investigation. One of the very first lessons a junior world defence agent must learn is to keep your eyes peeled at all times. That way, when your leader asks you questions in an emergency meeting about what you saw, you'll be able to give answers that are a whole lot more useful than "I didn't notice".

But it was OK. The good news was that while they were sitting in the queue, Harry and Colin had both had their eyes on Valentino.

"OK, guys," I said, pointing my pencil at the seed packet and getting ready to write. "Tell me about Valentino."

CHAPTER 3

"He had really hairy eyebrows," said Colin.

"How hairy?" I asked.

"Like hairy caterpillars," said Harry.

"What colour?" I asked.

"Brown," Harry added.

"I see." I frowned, writing *brown hairy caterpillars* on my seed packet. "What else do you remember?"

"He had at least two pairs of scissors in his pockets," said Colin.

"And he had an electric shaver," said Harry. "He went right over our heads with an electric shaver."

"And he made us wear a gown," said Colin.

"What type of gown?" I asked, reaching for another seed packet.

"A sort of black silky one," said Harry.

"With no arms," added Colin.

"No arms?" I frowned. "Did he tie you up to the chair with a rope before he made you put on the gown?" I asked.

"No," said Colin. "All he put on us was the gown."

"AND A RUBBER MAT!" gasped Harry. "He put a rubber mat on our shoulders too!"

"YOU'RE RIGHT!" gasped Colin. "I'd forgotten about the rubber mat!"

Clues were coming thick and fast now. I had used up one and a half seed packets, written down *brown hairy caterpillars, sharp scissors, electric shaver, gown with no arms,* and now *rubber mat.* This was getting interesting.

"Did he say anything to you when you were sitting down in the chair?" I asked.

"He asked lots of questions," said Harry.

"LOTS AND LOTS OF QUESTIONS!" Colin nodded.

"Such as?" I asked, getting them to remember each and every one:

1. Had we enjoyed the summer holiday?

2. Were we looking forward to going back to school?

3. What had we been doing during the summer holiday?

4. Had we been away anywhere on holiday?

5. Did we like football?

6. What team did we support?

These weren't questions. This was a full-on interrogation of my men. In broad daylight too. If Valentino was a real hairdresser, then I was a skateboarding elephant.

"Did you notice anything unusual after he had cut your hair?" I asked, reaching for seed packet number three.

"He sprinkled talcum powder on the back of our necks!" said Colin.

"And then he swept our hair up with A BROOM!" said Harry. "I remember looking round and seeing him do it. It was a red broom with a white handle!"

"And what did he do with all your hair once he had swept it up?" I asked.

"He put all of it into a giant bag!" said Colin.

"A great big see-through plastic bag!" Harry nodded.

"So he's collecting children's hair, is he?" I frowned, writing down *big bag of children's hair* and then giving it a double underline with my pencil.

It was time for a serious review of my notes.

CHAPTER 4

There is a skill to spotting danger. Not many people have it, but I do. If Valentino was a real hairdresser, then how come he was doing criminal haircuts? And if he was a criminal, why had he set up a pretend hairdresser's shop in the High Street?

From everything that Colin and Harry had told me it was clear that Valentino was up to no good:

1. Harry and Colin had been scalped by Valentino.

2. Harry and Colin had been interrogated by Valentino.
3. Harry and Colin had had their hair swept up by Valentino.
4. Taken away by Valentino.
5. And put into a big mysterious bag by Valentino.

If Valentino was up to something, then I needed to not only work out what it was but stop him in his evil tracks.

Two words kept jumping out at me from my notes. *Hairy* and *caterpillar*. "You say Valentino's eyebrows looked like brown hairy caterpillars. Do you think they could have actually *been* brown hairy caterpillars?" I asked.

Colin and Harry looked at each other and frowned.

"I mean, did you see them doing any wriggling when he was cutting your hair?" I asked.

"I didn't really notice," said Colin.

"Did they ever crawl higher up and onto his forehead, or down his nose or across his cheeks?" I asked.

Colin frowned. "I would definitely have noticed if they had!"

"They did go up and down quite a lot!" said Harry. "Especially when he was asking us questions!"

I had too many questions and not enough answers. There was only one thing for it. I needed to talk to the Intelligence Department at World Defence HQ and I needed to talk to them fast.

WORLD DEFENCE SECURITY TIP:

If you need to contact World Defence HQ fast to ask them important questions, make sure your left earlobe has been fitted with a two-way communication device. An invisible chip will arouse no suspicion and can be activated at any time by one press of your earlobe.

"Agent J to World Defence HQ. Over," I said. "Come in, World Defence HQ. Over . . .

"Intelligence Department please . . .

"Aha . . . suspicious activities . . .

"Ahum . . . in the High Street . . .

"Valentino . . .

"Aha . . .

"Ahum . . .

"Pretend hairdresser's shop . . .

"Completely scalped . . .

"Hairy caterpillars . . .

"Message received . . .

"Leave it to us!

"Emergency meeting over!" I shouted, jumping to my feet. "This isn't the work of a hairdresser, this is the work of a criminal mastermind!"

"What do you mean?" asked Colin, heading into the tunnel too.

"I mean, those furry things you spotted on Valentino's face this

40

morning weren't eyebrows at all –
they were SPYBROWS! ONLY AN
ENEMY AGENT WOULD USE
SPYBROWS!"

"SPYBROWS!?" gasped Harry.
"What are spybrows?"

"Spybrows are the very latest in enemy surveillance technology," I told him. "They look like hairy eyebrows, but really they are robot hairy caterpillars designed by Valentino to watch and record your every move!"

"You mean Valentino was using his eyebrows to spy on us all the time we were in the hairdresser's?"

"Exactly," I said. "Enemy HQ has probably found out that I'm training you to be junior world defence agents just like me, and has told Valentino to learn all our secrets."

"But why did he cut all our

hair off as well?" asked Harry. "Why didn't he just learn all our secrets and give us light trims?"

"Because the more children's hair he cuts off, the more robot hairy caterpillars he can make!" I said.

"THERE ARE MORE?" gasped Colin.

"There are more, all right." I nodded. "And I know just where to find them. Grab your bikes, follow me, and don't forget to put the lid back on the water butt!"

"Where are we going?" asked Harry.

"Half Moon Lane!" I shouted.

CHAPTER 5

I was kicking myself. I had discovered a ditch FULL of hairy caterpillars

just two evenings before, but it was only after seeing and hearing about Harry and Colin's haircuts that I'd realized my mistake. They weren't hairy caterpillars at all – they were SPYBROWS! The evidence was right in front of our eyes in the ditch at Half Moon Lane.

"This is what Valentino is making with your hair!" I whispered. "See here? He's using the hair from children's haircuts to create living, breathing, creeping, crawling enemy-agent spy gadgets!"

"There's hundreds of them!" said Harry, pointing at a long bramble stalk that was crawling with them. "They're eating the leaves! I didn't know robots ate leaves!"

"All part of the disguise," I told him. "Don't get too close. If they

jump at your face they could attach themselves to you for life!"

"How do they attach themselves?" asked Colin, leaning back sharply.

"They have special Velcro feet that can stick fast to human eyebrows," I said. "Once they're attached you can never shake them off."

"But why are there so many of them?" asked Harry.

"The more spy-brows Valentino makes, the more information he can

Spy brows

gather," I told him.

"Spybrows make pretty good moustaches as well actually," said Harry, hooking his finger over his top lip and grinning back at me and Colin.

"This is no laughing matter, Harry." I frowned. "What if Valentino's spybrows are just the tip of an evil hairy iceberg? What if Valentino has even bigger inventions planned?"

"There was an awful lot of hair in his bag," said Harry.

"He could make a hairy gorilla with the amount of hair he had in that bag!" said Colin.

"He could make a hairy mammoth!" said Harry with a chuckle.

Colin laughed too, but I didn't. What Harry had said was SeriouS with a capital S. At both ends.

"Back on your feet!" I shouted, leaping up from the grass and racing back to my bike.

"Where are we going now?" gasped Harry.

"Dino Valley!" I shouted. "Things are about to get even hairier!"

CHAPTER 6

Some of the best missions we've ever had have been at Dino Valley: dinosaur missions, caveman missions, sabre-toothed tiger missions, fungus-face fossil missions . . . I'm telling you, Dino Valley is one of the most dangerous places on earth. When you stand by the fence and look down into it, it kind of looks like a lumpy Sahara Desert with steeper sides. When you get to the bottom of the valley and look up, it's like being in a completely different world.

According to legend, Dino Valley was once a working quarry. Big yellow lorries used to drive back and forth out of the gates all day, carrying stones and sand to builders. But for two years now the big metal gates have been padlocked shut.

Some people say the stones and sand dried up, but I heard different.

Apparently, one day about two years ago, a massive digger was digging for gravel and sand in one of the oldest parts of the quarry when the grabber on the digger hit something hard. It was the giant stone door to a prehistoric world.

The man controlling the digger had no idea he had hit a secret door. All he heard was a clonk. Thinking it was just a big piece of stone, he raised the grabber higher and then brought it down again ten times harder.

This time there was more than a clonk – there was a *KERRANGGGG!!!* and then a *CRACK!!* and then a

SCREEEEAAAAMMMM! as the digger driver realized what he had done. But it was too late. Before he could turn the digger round, the door to the prehistoric world opened wide, a Tyrannosaurus Rex loomed out, grabbed him and ate him. And the digger. Then guess what? A Titanosaurus stomped out and ate the T. Rex!

No chewing, no nothing, just one great big gulp!

That very same day the quarry was closed for good and Dino Valley was born.

Dinosaurs have roamed the valley

ever since and people have totally stayed away. Apart from me, Colin and Harry. Nothing can stop a junior world defence agent and his men from entering Dino Valley. Especially when there is a big hole in the fence.

We got to Dino Valley just after 15:00 hundred hours. Colin was the

first one to squeeze through, then me. We needed two pairs of hands to pull the wire back far enough to get our bikes through the hole, but once Harry had lifted them through and then climbed through himself, we were almost good to go.

Bikes camouflaged, we stared down at the valley floor.

WORLD DEFENCE DINOSAUR-APPROACH TIP:

Always camouflage your bikes before entering dinosaur territory. Otherwise they might get eaten.

"OK, men," I said. "If Valentino has the evil scientific skills to turn hair from children's haircuts into spybrows, then evil, rampaging hairy mammoths could definitely be part of his plan too."

"Why don't you ask World Defence HQ if they've seen any signs of them?" asked Harry.

Colin nodded. "If they have, they might be able to give us some hairy mammoth defence tips."

Colin and Harry were learning fast. World Defence HQ had the satellite technology to give us all the information we needed.

"Agent J to World Defence HQ. Over," I said, giving my earlobe another squeeze. "Do you copy? Over.

"Yes, spybrows located, Half Moon Lane . . .

"Now arrived, Dino Valley . . . Valentino . . . Enemy agent, yes . . . Hairy mammoths . . .

"Dangerous? How dangerous . . . ?

"Hairy? How hairy . . . !?

"Powerful? How powerful . . . !!?

"Masterplan? What masterplan . . . ?

"WORLD? THE ENTIRE WORLD . . . ?!

"Message received. Leave it to us!!!"

CHAPTER 7

There was good news and bad news. The good news was, World Defence HQ had sent planes to sprinkle Half Moon Lane with Velcro grass seed. As soon as it began to grow, the feet of every single spybrow would be stuck fast to the Velcro blades. Valentino's spybrows wouldn't be going anywhere.

The bad news was, Valentino's hairy mammoths weren't just on the rampage, they were more hairy and more dangerous than I'd ever imagined; so dangerous that I could hardly bring myself to tell Colin and Harry the awful truth. In fact I decided it was better not to tell them anything until we had reached the valley floor.

Going back in time is one of the most dangerous things a world

defence agent can ever do, especially at Dino Valley.

It was 15:11 hundred hours AD when we started our climb from the top and almost 15:21 hundred hours BC when we arrived at the bottom. That's the way Dino Valley works – the lower you climb, the further back in time you go. The moment you put your foot down on the valley floor, everything turns prehistoric.

"Are you ready to turn into cavemen?" I shouted, just one footstep from the bottom.

"WE are!" cheered Harry and Colin.

"Then get ready to turn into cavemen!" I shouted.

STONE-AGE TRANSFORMATION!

The instant we turned into cavemen, I set about briefing Colin and Harry.

"Listen," I told them, putting both hands to my ears. "Can you hear that?"

"Hear what?" asked Harry.

"The sound of prehistoric hair-dryers." I frowned. "According to World Defence HQ, Valentino hasn't just been making hairy mammoths, he's been using evil hairdressing technology to create the most dangerous type of hairy mammoth the world has ever seen!"

"How do you mean?" gasped Colin.

"I mean, instead of his mammoths having normal trunks, they've got massive hairy hairdryers for trunks instead!"

"HAIRY HAIRDRYERS FOR TRUNKS!!" Harry shuddered.

"MASSIVE hairy hairdryers for trunks." I nodded. "But that's not all.

Each trunk has the power of a hundred hairdryers! Switched to maximum, they can blow away anything that stands in their path: trees, bushes, boulders, mountains, T. Rexes . . . !"

"Us," gulped Colin.

"How are we going to stand up to mammoths that have got massive hairdrying trunks?" gasped Harry.

"We'll just have to," I told him. "Because if we don't, Valentino will use his hairy creations to take over the ENTIRE WORLD!"

"THE ENTIRE WORLD!" gasped Colin. "BUT HOW!?"

CHAPTER 8

Like all mad scientists' plans,
Valentino's weren't just evil, they
were evil genius.

"HQ says that Valentino has
programmed his hairy mammoths
to blow away everything in their

path," I told Colin and Harry, "starting with Dino Valley and then moving on to the outside world."

"The outside world?" said Harry. "But that's where we live!"

"It won't be if Valentino gets his evil way," I told them. "If Valentino's mammoths get out of Dino Valley, they will blow away every building on the planet: every house, every office, every tower block, every tepee, every igloo, every palace, every mud hut, every tent, even every cave. When they've finished, there will be no places to live anywhere on the planet."

"But why would Valentino want to do that?" asked Colin.

"Because there is a new Ice Age coming," I told him, "and when it hits, humans will need places to live in and keep warm."

"Like homes and buildings!" said Harry.

"Homes and buildings with central heating." I nodded. "No homes, no shelter; no shelter, no warmth."

"No warmth, no humans!" gasped Colin.

"No humans except Valentino." I frowned. "If his evil plan works, the

ICE-AGE DESTRUCTION!

NO WARMTH, NO HUMANS!

HUMAN ANNIHILATION!

NO HUMANS EXCEPT VALENTINO!

planet will be turned into one giant snowball. Valentino will be the only one left, which means he will have total control of the entire world."

"But how will Valentino survive the new Ice Age?" asked Harry. "If the temperatures are so cold and

there is nowhere to live, how will he manage to keep warm?"

"Super-hairy Ice-Age-proof thermal suits," I told them. "Valentino's been using his bag of hairs to make hairy clothing too."

"Is there anything hairy he can't make from his evil haircuts?" gasped Colin.

"I'm afraid not," I told them. "He is a total evil genius and he has to be stopped!"

"When will the new Ice Age arrive?" asked Harry.

"According to HQ, in about an hour and a half," I said, "so we're going to have to work fast!"

WORLD DEFENCE WEAPON-MAKING TIP:

Use things in the environment to craft awesome mission-winning weapons.

CHAPTER 9

As soon as my Stone-Age briefing was over, we set about making our essential caveman weapons.

Luckily there was a bush we could chop bits off, pieces of wood we could carve and a long piece of caveman string left over from a prehistoric tug-of-war.

In no time at all, we had all the Stone-Age weaponry we could ever need!

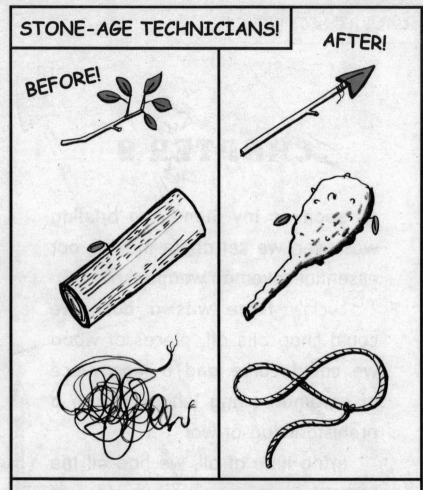

STONE-AGE TECHNICIANS!

BEFORE!

AFTER!

THE THREE BRAVE CAVEMEN WORKED TIRELESSLY TO CREATE AWESOME WEAPONS. THERE WAS NOTHING THEY COULDN'T MAKE AND NOTHING THEY COULDN'T TACKLE.

It was a forty-mile trek to the hairy mammoths' lair. After a quarter of an hour of really fast marching, our food supplies had already begun to run low.

"Eat stones," I told Harry and Colin after twenty minutes of crawling. After five more minutes, our water bottles were completely empty.

"Suck stones," I told them. "And if you see a dinosaur, try and drink its sweat . . . without it seeing," I added.

Without my survival knowledge, we would have died for sure, but with it, nothing could stop us.

SUPPLIES LOW.

CRUEL SUN.

The sound of distant hairdryers had been growing louder with our every step, and I was certain that trouble would soon be looming.

"Rest here for a moment," I commanded, licking my finger and then holding it up above my head to check the breeze.

Something in the air had changed.

WORLD DEFENCE SURVIVAL TIP:
Use finger-sucking skills to check changes in wind speed and direction.

Not only was the sound of hairdryers growing louder – the breeze from the hairdryers was growing stronger too!

"How long till we see them?" asked Colin.

"Sharpen your spears, raise your clubs!" I shouted. "They're about to catch up with us NOW!!"

CHAPTER 10

The moment we turned the corner of the valley, the sound of hurricane-force hairdryers filled the air.

"On your feet!" I shouted, as a herd of about fifty hairdrying mammoths came stampeding straight towards us with their trunks switched to maximum power.

"Shield your eyes!" I shouted, as the mammoths got up close. "If they dry out our eyeballs, we'll go blind!"

Our weapons were poised, but the force of the mammoths' trunks was off the scale. Massive dinosaurs were flying straight over our heads and boulders were whistling past our ears!

"Hold your nerve!" I yelled, standing tall and then aiming my spear. "Aim right between their eyes!" I commanded, wrenching my spear back and then throwing it with all my strength.

Colin and Harry followed my lead, but it was no good. Our spears just blew away like leaves in the wind.

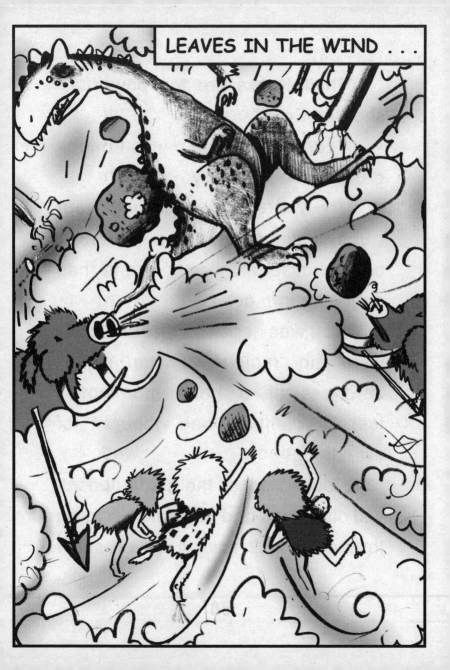

"Their trunks are too powerful!" shouted Colin.

"I can barely keep my feet on the ground!" yelled Harry.

"Try and get in close with your clubs," I shouted, doing a triple roly-poly across the valley floor and then springing into action.

But it was hopeless. Our weapons were no match for the super-hardness of a hairy mammoth's tusks. Valentino had thought of everything!

I looked up at the sky. It wasn't just dinosaurs and boulders whizzing through the air now. A full-on snow

THREAT OF EXTINCTION!

blizzard had started too!

"THE ICE AGE IS COMING! Just as HQ warned!" I pointed. "Look at the sky. In about two minutes the whole of the planet will be frozen!"

"If the planet freezes, we'll freeze too," gasped Harry.

"Stand firm!" I commanded. "It's time to show these hairy mammoths what junior world defence agents are made of!"

CHAPTER 11

Our spears were lost and our clubs were in pieces. The only weapon we had left was a lasso!

Could I lasso a mammoth? No way.

Could I tie up a mammoth with a lasso? No way.

Could I trip up a mammoth with a lasso? No way.

But could I stop a mammoth with a lasso? Yes way!

By changing it into a slingshot!

"Pterodactyl eggs!" I shouted. "Fetch me as many Pterodactyl eggs as you can find!"

Colin and Harry raced off to find Pterodactyl eggs while I untied the knot on my lasso.

"What are you going to do with them?" panted Harry, racing back with a prehistoric wheelbarrow full of giant eggs.

As soon as I had finished retying my rope into a slingshot, I loaded it with my first Pterodactyl egg.

"Slingshot skills," I shouted. "Watch and learn!

"Take that!" I shouted, firing my first giant egg straight down the end of a mammoth's trunk.

"Bullseye!!!!!" I whooped, swinging my slingshot around my head and doing a caveman victory dance.

The first mammoth's eyes bulged BIG TIME and its cheeks began to blow up like a balloon.

"Double bullseye!" I yelled, as my second egg blocked another hairdrying trunk like a cork.

"Forty-eight more to go!" Harry shouted, handing me my third egg.

"Triple bullseye!" I cheered, firing my third egg straight down the trunk of another mammoth.

Colin and Harry were really impressed with my slingshot skills, but the hairy mammoths were furious. In fact the angrier they got, the hotter their hairdryers became!

"LOOK, THEY'RE OVERHEATING!" I yelled, watching the snow start to drip from their hairy bodies. "Fetch me more ammo fast!"

Harry and Colin knew just where to look.

"Keep 'em coming!" I shouted. "Keep 'em coming!!!!"

Egg by egg, mammoth by mammoth, my slingshot skills did the business. The harder the hairdrying mammoths tried to unblock their trunks, the more overheated they became! The more overheated they became, the more their hairy bodies started to inflate!

"They're floating into the air!" gasped Colin, raising his snowy arm and pointing.

"They can't keep their feet on the ground!" cheered Harry.

Colin and Harry were right. Victory was ours, but the battle was only half won.

"How are we going to stop the freezing power of a new Ice Age?!" I shivered.

All around us the blizzard was worsening. A full-on Ice Age was only milliseconds away now and the world was fast turning to ice.

"If the world turns to ice, we'll turn to ice too!" gulped Colin.

"My eyeballs have frozen!" gasped Harry, staggering around with total snow blindness.

"Mine too," groaned Colin, dropping to his knees. "Jack, you're going to have to save the world on your own!"

There are times in a world defence agent's life when you can rely on your survival skills and there are times when you have to trust to plain luck. Defeating hairy hairdrying mammoths single-handed was one thing, but stopping a new Ice Age from freezing the planet was a task that even I didn't have the skills for.

Luckily, luck was on our side.

"Cover your ears!" I shouted.

Colin and Harry dropped down onto the snow and covered their ears as the herd of floating mammoths suddenly exploded with the heat of five thousand hairdryers! It wasn't just luck, it was a full-on prehistoric miracle!

MIRACLE THAW!

The heat from the hairdryers was more than enough to melt everything back to normal and stop the Ice Age from happening for at least another million years. Three cavemen – but mostly me – had saved the world with nothing more than a slingshot and a barrow-load of Pterodactyl eggs! Even with my mission skills and experience I could barely believe it.

"I can see!" shouted Colin, instantly getting his sight back.

"Me too!" cheered Harry.

Harry and Colin were right to be pleased, because although I was basically the one who had saved the world, I would never have been able to do it if they hadn't found the Pterodactyl eggs.

It was 17:17 hundred hours BC by the time we had finished our caveman celebrations, and 17:25 by the time we had headed back to our bikes.

In the space of just one day, our amazing teamwork had stopped hairy spybrows, hairy hairdrying mammoths and even a new Ice Age.

"Where are we going next?" Colin asked.

"Valentino's shop." I smiled. "Before it closes at six o'clock!"

CHAPTER 12

I wasn't christened Jack "Dragon" Beechwhistle. I chose the Dragon bit myself. Most of the children in my class at school have middle names; some even have two middle names. My mum and dad didn't have time to think of a middle name for me, so I decided I'd come up with something for myself.

Dragons are my favourite animals. I like dragons because they have no fear. Even if they couldn't breathe fire I reckon they would have no fear; you can see it in their eyes.

Having no fear is an essential part of being a world defence agent, even a junior one. Especially when you're on a mission that takes you right into the heart of enemy territory.

I had never actually been into a hairdresser's shop in my life. My mum has always cut my hair at home with the kitchen scissors. But to get the information I needed, I had no choice.

I had decided that when we got to Valentino's, I would let Harry and Colin stay outside the shop. They

112

had already suffered enough at the hands of Valentino and the hairy mammoths, and anyway I needed them to guard the bikes.

When I told Harry and Colin that we were going to Valentino's, I think they thought I was going to get my hair cut too. But that wasn't my plan at all. My plan was to walk in, wait in the queue, watch Valentino's every move and then run out before it was my turn to sit down in his chair. That way I could see precisely what he was up to and see exactly how big that big bag of hair truly was.

At least, that was my plan.

We arrived outside Valentino's at 17:51 hundred hours. Just nine minutes before closing.

The problem was, when I walked into the shop it was empty, which meant there was no one in the queue or the chair. Plus the stupid bell above the door rang, so Valentino noticed me straight away.

"Take a seat!" Valentino said, before I had a chance to even think about escaping.

The moment he flapped his gown at me, I knew I had an impossible choice – give up on my investigation or take a hit for the team. As a leader of men, I had no choice but to lead. I gritted my teeth. I sat down on the chair. And I let Valentino do his worst.

Valentino was a pro. He had a couple of pairs of scissors and two combs in his pockets. And those were just the evil instruments I could see. I wouldn't have been surprised if he'd even more tucked into his socks. Before you could say "snip", he had me exactly where he wanted me, gown on, seat adjusted, rubber mat weighing me down.

"What would you like?" he asked, pressing both hands down on my shoulders and staring at my reflection in the mirror.

His eyebrows definitely looked like hairy caterpillars. He even had hairy caterpillars poking out of his ears.

"An extremely light trim," I told him. "An extremely, really, really light trim – just a bit off the back – nowhere else please."

But it was hopeless. Valentino wasn't interested in anything I had to say. He didn't care what haircut I wanted at all. All he wanted to do was sit me in his evil seat, take his evil scissors out of his evil pocket and do his evil worst. I might just as well have answered, "I'll have a baldie please, Valentino," because that's exactly what I got.

"You like?" he asked me, holding up a mirror and moving it from both sides of my head to the back.

"Very nice, thanks," I said, not wanting him to know who he was dealing with.

On any other mission, I would have got out of there, and got out fast. But I needed to see what Valentino was going to do with my chopped-off hair. Would he sweep it up like Harry had said? And if so, would he add it to the giant bag that Colin and Harry had seen?

I didn't have to wait long to find out.

CHAPTER 13

The instant I climbed out of the hairdresser's chair, Valentino slipped the rubber mat and gown off my shoulders and shook all my snips of hair onto the floor. Then, without a word of warning, he turned and disappeared out of sight.

I was alone for two seconds. All three seed packets were still in my jeans pocket, and when Valentino returned from the room at the back of his shop, I had my emergency meeting notes at the ready.

Colin's description of Valentino's broom had been spot on. It was red at the sweeping end and had a long white handle. It came with a matching dustpan and brush too.

Then I saw the bag!

Red hair, brown hair, blond hair, black hair, long hair, short hair, curly hair, frizzy hair, Colin's hair, Harry's hair – and now MY HAIR! I had no idea there had been so many victims before me!!

But then things got really serious.

"Four pounds fifty, please," Valentino said, leaning his broom against the wall and putting the dustpan and brush on top of his big bulging bag.

Four pounds fifty? I thought. *For a scalping?* I had never imagined that he would actually ask me to pay!

But Valentino wasn't joking. He was deadly serious. His eyes were staring straight at me, his spybrows raised, his arm out and the palm of his hand open.

I looked at his evil fingers. They were the fingers that had scalped a thousand scalps. Even if I'd had any money, even if I'd had 10p – even if I'd had 5p – even if I'd had 1p – there was no way I would have put it into Valentino's mitts.

WORLD DEFENCE ESCAPE TIP:
If you're cornered by a hairdresser who isn't a real hairdresser, but he's asking you for real money, RUN!

So I ran!
Head down.
Nerves jangling.
I was out of there in a FLASH!

CHAPTER 14

I had never run out of a shop without paying before! My heart was absolutely blamming as I raced through the door.

"LEG IT!" I shouted the moment I saw Colin and Harry. "I haven't paid!"

As soon as they realized that Valentino was after me, they stopped grinning at my haircut and grabbed their bikes.

"I'LL CALL THE POLICE!" shouted

Valentino, as he burst through the door with his eyebrows out of control.

WORLD DEFENCE SUPER-FAST ESCAPE TIP:
For super-fast escapes make sure your bike can switch to emergency total-turbo motorbike power.

We needed to escape and we needed to escape FAST! Luckily, our bikes had a nifty trick up their sleeves.

"TURBO TIME!" I shouted.

WHEELIES OF WONDER!

CORNERS OF COURAGE!

Our total-turbo-driving skills were more than a match for Valentino – there was no way he could ever catch us on our bikes. Down the High Street, through the park and across Scorched Urf we sped. Hoods up, heads down, tyres smoking, we were probably halfway home before Valentino had stopped shaking his fist!

"YAHOOO!" cheered Colin.

"HAVE WE LOST HIM?!" gasped Harry, screeching to a halt outside his front gate.

"TAKE COVER!" I shouted, pointing up at the sky. "He's chasing us in a helicopter!"

It was true. A helicopter was totally hovering in the sky above us, and there was no doubt in my mind that it was Valentino.

WORLD DEFENCE TIP:
If you are being chased by the enemy in a helicopter, jump off your bike, cover yourself with camouflage and lie low.

Thank goodness we had Bunker H to hide in!

Bunker H is the emergency underground bunker in Harry's back garden. We built it in case of an alien attack. Big enough for me, Colin and Harry and all three of our bikes to get under, it was perfect as a hiding place now.

"OK, men," I said, taking total command. "Lie perfectly still and breathe only if you have to."

"I need to pant!" gasped Colin.

"Me too," gulped Harry. "I've never been so puffed out!"

"Then pant quietly," I ordered. "I can only lead you to safety if you do exactly as I say!"

RACE FOR COVER!

"Valentino must be pretty angry to chase us in a helicopter," whispered Colin.

"I think he's going!" said Harry, high-fiving Colin as the helicopter passed overhead.

"Just because we can't see him doesn't mean he isn't there," I told them. "If his helicopter has long-range listening devices, then he could be parked up behind a cloud waiting to hear what our next move is."

"Do you think he has called the police?" whispered Colin.

"No way," I said. "He won't want the police sniffing around his evil operation."

THE THREE MEN LAY LOW AS THE EVIL
HELICOPTER PASSED OVERHEAD.

"You don't think his helicopter fires missiles, do you?" whispered Harry, poking his head out of our bunker and peering up at the sky.

"Probably," I said. "But if it does, our force fields will deflect them."

"And if they don't deflect his missiles, we'll just dodge them." Colin smiled.

"Maybe we'll just catch the missiles and throw them straight back at him!" laughed Harry.

"Too right!" I nodded, but there was no need to worry. At 18:47 hundred hours, I gave the all clear.

CHAPTER 15

We had escaped Valentino's helicopter, but we hadn't defeated Valentino. He had Colin's hair in his bag. He had Harry's hair in his bag. And now he had topped it up with my hair too.

Was it possible that he was up to something EVEN BIGGER?

"I wish we knew where Valentino lived," I said, crawling out of Bunker H on my hands and knees and double-checking the sky. "If we knew where he lived, we could check out his house and his laboratories."

"I know where he lives," said Harry, following me out and then jumping to his feet. "My cousin Jeremy delivered a newspaper to his house once."

"Why didn't you tell me before?" I gasped.

WORLD DEFENCE IMPORTANT INFORMATION TIP:
Never withhold important information, especially if it's key to the success of a mission.

"I forgot," said Harry. "And anyway, you didn't ask."

"So where does he live then?" I asked.

"On the Millsham Lodge Estate," Harry continued. "Maple Avenue, last house on the left before the first bend. Valentino told Jeremy off for delivering his newspaper 'American style'."

"What's 'American style'?" asked Colin.

"It's when you throw the newspaper at the front door instead of posting it through the letter box," said Harry. "It was the first day of

Jeremy's paper round. Valentino was coming out of his front door that morning just as Jeremy threw it."

"Did it hit him?" I asked.

Harry shook his head. "Not exactly. If you're going to do a paper round 'American style', I think you're meant to put rubber bands around the newspapers after you've rolled them up to hold them together. Jeremy didn't have any rubber bands."

"So what happened?" asked Colin.

"Valentino's newspaper kind of fell apart and then blew all over his garden," said Harry. "Apparently the crossword ended up in a puddle. Valentino went mental. And he reported my cousin to the newsagent."

"What did the newsagent say?" I asked.

"He gave Jeremy the sack," said Harry. "After one day."

"What, all because of one measly newspaper?" asked Colin.

"Not exactly," said Harry. "He'd
been delivering his newspapers
'American style' to five other streets
before he got to Valentino's. I think

there were newspapers in puddles everywhere."

"No wonder he knows where Valentino lives," I said, pulling a seed packet out of my back pocket and adding the enemy scientist's address to my notes.

"Jeremy refuses to get his hair cut at Valentino's now," Harry added.

"I don't blame him!" I said, rubbing my hand over my scalped scalp.

It was only seven o'clock, but before I could even point us in the direction of our next mission our day was suddenly ended by shouts from Harry and Colin's mums.

It was time for them to go in for their dinner.

And their bath.

And then bed.

It was the same every night for Colin and Harry: bed at eight o'clock, EVEN in the school holidays!

"If we know where Valentino lives, why don't we check out his house tomorrow?" said Colin, dragging his bike out of Bunker H and then wheeling it across Harry's back lawn. "It will be Saturday, so he won't even be at home, he'll be at work!"

"We can sneak into his garden and look through his windows and everything!" said Harry.

Harry and Colin were learning fast. They had already guessed where the next day's mission would be.

"OK, men," I said. "We will meet outside Harry's house tomorrow morning at nine o'clock sharp. We'll have a breakfast briefing in our secret den at 09:30 hundred hours – sooner if we can."

We always have breakfast briefings in our secret den on Saturday mornings. It's totally the best way to prepare for dangerous weekend missions.

"Colin, bread. Harry, sauce. I'll bring the bacon," I said, wheeling my bike through Harry's front gate and then crossing the road to my house.

"Will do!" they shouted.

"Goodness, that's short!" I heard Harry's mum gasp as Harry went inside.

"Ooh, my word!" shrieked Colin's mum as she saw Colin's haircut for the first time too. "You've been scalped!"

"I only asked for a light trim!" moaned Colin as he disappeared through the front door.

 *I didn't even ask for that*, I thought, giving my head an unlucky rub.

There were no two ways about it: Valentino had a lot to answer for and I was determined to see that he answered for it big time.

As I watched the front doors to Harry and Colin's houses close, my tummy began to rumble. All that talk of bacon sandwiches had really got my juices going. It was time I headed home for dinner too!

Well, it was time I headed home.

CHAPTER 16

My mum doesn't really do dinner during the week. She sometimes does takeaways, but when she and Dad get back from the pub, I'm usually in bed. Sometimes I have what's left for my breakfast.

My house was empty when I got in. It's always empty on a Friday night. Actually it's empty most nights because my mum and dad need to go down the pub.

My dad has to go down the pub much more than he wants to, for important World Defence Agency business. My mum has to go with him an awful lot too, just to cover his back.

Once I went down to the pub car park to see if I could see them through the window. But when my dad saw me, he came outside and told me I needed to go home straight away. Apparently the pub was full of enemy agents and he was worried they might work out that I'd been recruited to be a world defence agent too.

I've kind of got used to being on my own in the house now.

The best thing about being on your own in the house is you can choose anything that you want for dinner! Provided you can find it in the fridge or the cupboards and provided you can cook it.

There were only three pieces of bacon in the fridge when I looked, and I would need those for my meeting with Colin and Harry the next morning. There were lots of lagers, but I'm not allowed to drink those, and there was a piece of chicken that didn't smell very nice.

The cereal boxes I looked in were empty and the things in the freezer would take ages to thaw.

In the end I decided to have bread.

The good thing about bread is you can eat it raw, which is brilliant because I couldn't find any butter either. Learning to eat things raw is a key survival skill, especially if you're lost on a mission and there's no way of doing any cooking.

The other good thing about bread is it's already sliced.

The bread I made that Friday was delicious. I

ate about five slices before I even sat down!

My house sounds really quiet when I'm sitting indoors on my own. That evening it was so quiet I could hear every chew of my bread.

Instead of putting on the telly, I decided to sit by the window. I had thinking to do – serious thinking – about what Valentino had been up to and what he might be up to next.

Harry was definitely right. Valentino had added my hair to his evil collection now. What if he was already using my hair

to invent something even hairier?
What if his house had bags of hair
piled up in every room? There would
be no limit to his hairy evilness!

There was definitely more
investigating that needed to be done.

If Valentino was on the verge of something super-duper hairy, then before I got Colin and Harry involved again, I needed to work out exactly how dangerous our next mission might be. I needed to map out Valentino's garden, assess his security systems and, if possible, get a sneaky look through his windows.

Not only that, I needed to do it solo.

It was 20:22 hundred hours and the light was fading fast.

I finished my bread and walked up the stairs.

It was time to put on my shadow gear.

CHAPTER 17

By 20:37 hundred hours I was back on my bike and heading for town.

Black balaclava, black hoodie, black T-shirt, black scarf, black jeans, black socks, black trainers, black gloves. My shadow gear is perfect for night-time operations.

Shadow missions are totally different to daylight missions because everything you do is in the dark. That's what makes them the best.

My bike is totally equipped for shadow missions. Not only has it got a white light at the front and a red light at the back – both lights do three different types of flashing:

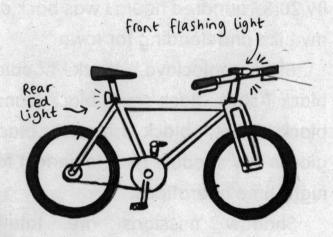

front flashing light

Rear red light →

1. Not flashing.
2. Flashing.
3. Really flashing.

Having a bike with flashing lights is really important when you're a junior world defence agent because it means you can send out emergency signals to other agents. Plus they look really cool.

As soon as I reached the end of my street I stopped and adjusted the strap on my helmet. I forgot to mention  my helmet: it's black, like the rest of my shadow gear. It gets a bit tight when I'm wearing my balaclava underneath, but it gives me brilliant protection if I crash in a high-speed chase or have to weave my way through unexpected dangers. Night or day.

I knew exactly how to get to Valentino's house because my auntie and uncle live on the Millsham Lodge Estate too. Maple Avenue is on the way to their house. In fact I had passed Valentino's house in my dad's car more times than I'd ever realized.

I had decided to cycle mostly on the pavement, but switch to the road when I got to the High Street. Grown-ups in high streets don't like

you cycling on the pavement, e s p e c i a l l y when they are walking along in big groups. I know, because I crashed into someone once.

It took me about fifteen minutes to reach town. It was busy even for a Friday night: cars were trying to park and people were trying to cross the road. I just kept my head down and my bike lights flashing.

The moment I turned off the High Street, I jumped my tyres back onto the pavement. The instant I reached the estate, I dropped my shoulders low.

WORLD DEFENCE CYCLING TIP:
Always keep a low profile when approaching an enemy agent's house. If there are secret security cameras on the approach roads, he might take your photo and share it with enemy HQ.

All the streets on the Millsham Lodge Estate are named after trees. Don't ask me why, they just are. If I

got the chance to name streets, I'd name them after dinosaurs – you know, Stegosaurus Street, Allosaurus Avenue, Diplodocus Drive and stuff like that. Dinosaurs are a hundred times cooler than trees; mind you,

I'm not sure I'd like to try and climb one.

Away from the town the streets were much quieter – so quiet I was almost afraid to use my brakes. On a shadow mission, the squeak of a brake can be the difference between success and failure. Luckily I'd oiled them the morning before.

Holly Way was the first road I turned into. Then Larch Grove, Sycamore Way and Cypress Drive.

The further I cycled, the faster my heart began to beat. I had done hundreds of shadow missions before, but nothing as hairy as this.

By 21:07, I had Maple Avenue in my sights. Five seconds later I was within sniffing distance of Valentino's house.

WORLD DEFENCE NIGHT-TIME SURVEILLANCE TIP:
Use the cover of darkness to help you with your night-time mission. Obscure the enemy's vision by staying close to trees, bushes or garden walls. Above all, remember to turn your bike lights off.

I had seen no obvious signs of danger as I'd cycled through the

estate, but as I climbed off my saddle and flicked the switches on my lights, I was sure that danger would be looming now.

Like all ingeniously disguised enemy houses, Valentino's house looked no different from any other in the street. It had a driveway, it had a front lawn, it had windows and a front door, but I was far too experienced to be fooled by that.

What else did it have?

What else was Valentino hiding?

I was totally about to find out.

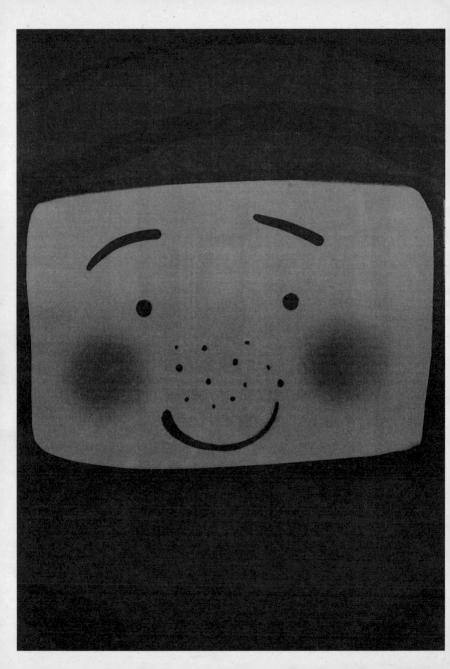

CHAPTER 18

I don't know if you have ever spied on someone's house in the dark before, but it's something that takes a bit of practice. The first time you creep into someone's garden in the dark, loads of things go through your mind. *Will they see me? Will they chase me? Will I get caught?*

Most of my early tryouts were in my own road. While my mum and dad were down the pub, I would climb over my fence and see how many back gardens I could creep through without being seen. In my earliest practices I would only ever manage to do two, because as soon as someone in a house turned towards the window, I thought they were looking straight at me.

But they weren't. That's one of the weird and brilliant things you learn about shadow work. If it's night-time and the lights are on in a house, you can see the people inside, but the people inside can't see you! Just cross your fingers and hope there aren't any security lights.

Security lights are your biggest chance of being spotted on a shadow mission: security lights, security guards and infra-red night-time vision cameras. I was sure Valentino would have all of those.

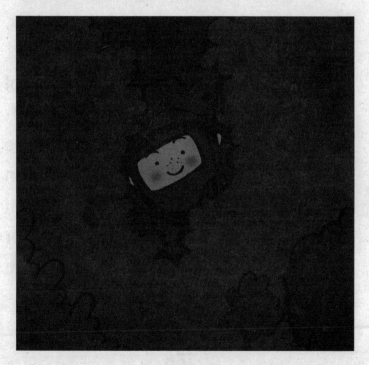

With a deep breath, I pushed my head through one of Valentino's bushes and parted the leaves with my gloves. At 21:09 hundred hours, I decided to make my move.

I was in luck. The lights were on in Valentino's front room and, even better, the curtains were open.

There were no obvious signs of security lights, security guards or night-vision surveillance cameras, but there were two rows of suspicious garden lights running up the path to the front door. Were they real garden lights or did they have invisible laser-beam tripwires? It was impossible to tell.

To keep myself super safe, I decided to take a different approach to Valentino's house.

At 21:11 hundred hours, I ducked low, raced to the far corner of Valentino's garden . . .

. . . then jumped over his wall and landed on his front lawn.

Two shadow roly-polys later, I was back on my feet, with my back pressed to his hedge.

From where I was standing, I couldn't see properly into Valentino's front room. All I could see was the top

of a chair, quite a lot of wallpaper and a doorway that I guessed led into his hall.

I needed to get to the window ledge for a proper front-on view.

I counted to ten, took a deep breath and then did six more shadow roly-polys across Valentino's front lawn. It was a brilliant manoeuvre, combining speed with ninja-style agility. As soon as I reached the wall of his house, I turned, adjusted my helmet and then froze. A car was coming down the road with its headlights on!

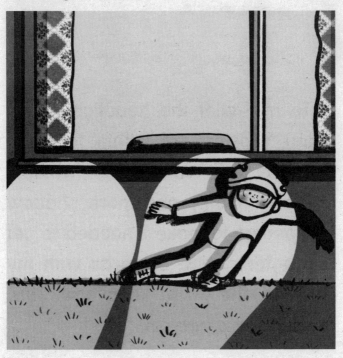

WORLD DEFENCE SPOTLIGHT-AVOIDANCE TIP:

If you are caught in a spotlight during a shadow mission, don't move a muscle.

To my relief the headlights kept going, leaving me within touching distance of Valentino's window ledge with only one more shadow manoeuvre to make. I needed to get to my feet, slide upwards with my back to the wall, keep low, turn my head and peep in.

Here goes, I thought, sliding my back up towards the sill.

Oh no, I thought, turning my head and inching my eyes up towards the window.

In the time it had taken me to get to the window, duck down and bob up, Valentino had drawn his curtains. Now I couldn't see anything at all!

I needed a Plan B and I needed one fast.

WORLD DEFENCE MISSION PLAN A TIP:
Always have a Plan B.

If Valentino had drawn his curtains, maybe I could peep through the gap where they met.

But there was no gap. The curtains had completely overlapped.

My Plan C was good enough to be a Plan A. And I was in luck. Valentino did have a letter box, plus there were no laser tripwires on his path, no security lights in his front porch, and his front doormat wasn't booby-trapped either.

The coast was clear!

Quiet as a shadow, invisible as a ⬛⬛⬛⬛, I crept up to Valentino's door, crouched down on the doormat, and got ready to see exactly what he was doing inside that house.

Slowly, carefully, I reached up with my hand, stiffened my fingers and pushed the letter box open . . .

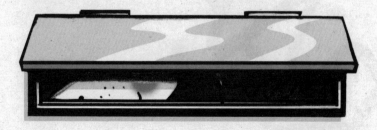

RAAAAAAA

HRAHROOOAARR

SUDDENLY, from out of nowhere, there was a roaring monster just inches from my glove!

It had teeth, it had hair and, from the sound of it, it had an appetite not just for my fingers but for the rest of me too!

My eyeballs popped and my heart exploded!

It was time to . . .

RUN

WORLD DEFENCE RAPID-RETREAT TIP: If you are suddenly faced with an enemy of superior height, weight, ferocity and hairiness, abort your mission immediately.

I was back on my bike faster than you could ping a rubber band. I was at the end of Maple Avenue quicker than you can say 'qu'!!!! I was halfway down the High Street before I even remembered to switch my lights back on!

It was supersonic turbo time!

203

The instant I skidded onto the driveway of my house, I dropped my bike, raced into the kitchen and ran up to my bedroom. My mum and dad were still out, which was good really, because I wouldn't have wanted to frighten them.

Of all the enemy agents I had ever come up against, Valentino was easily the worst. Valentino's evilness was off the scale.

He had used his evil haircuts to invent spybrows.

He had used evil hairdressing technology to invent hairy hairdrying mammoths.

And now, from the look and sound of things, he had used his scientific evilness to invent the hairiest horror of them all!

But what was it?

How hairy was it?

How evil was it?

And how HUNGRY was it?

One thing was for certain: Valentino and his hairy horror had to be stopped.

Two things *weren't* for certain. Would Colin and Harry be up to the job?

CHAPTER 19

On Saturday morning, Harry and Colin were bang on time, as usual. We were on our bikes by five past nine and cooking bacon in our secret den by 09:25 hundred hours.

Before I went to bed on Friday, I had given Valentino's address

to World Defence HQ and asked them to keep his house under close surveillance overnight. I was sure that by Saturday morning the Satellite Technology Department would have all the answers I needed.

I decided to let Harry and Colin eat their breakfast before telling them about the shadow mission I had done the night before. Firstly, I wanted them to enjoy their bacon. Secondly, I wasn't sure how they would react when I told them how dangerous our next mission was going to be.

"What did you see?" asked Harry, wiping sandwich crumbs and tomato sauce off his lips.

"It's not what I saw, it's what I didn't see." I frowned, lowering my voice to let them know that what I was about to say was deadly serious. "I only had a letter box to look through."

"What didn't you see?" gasped Colin.

"I'm about to ask that very same question," I said, pressing my earlobe and making instant radio contact with World Defence HQ.

"Agent J to World Defence HQ, are you receiving me? Over . . .

"Receiving you loud and clear. Over . . .

"Aha, ahum . . .

"Valentino, yes . . . 73 Maple Avenue, yes . . . Shadow mission, yes . . . Letter box, yes . . . Narrow escape . . .

"Aha, ahum . . .

"Ahum, aha . . .

"He's invented WHAT?

"The HAIRY HORROR FROM WHERE . . . !!!!????!!!

"HOW BIG . . . !?

"HOW HAIRY . . . !?

"HOW EVIL . . . !?

"HOW HUNGRY . . . !?

"Aha, oh no . . .

"END OF THE WORLD!!

"END OF THE UNIVERSE!!!!!

"Message received. LEAVE IT TO US!!!! Over."

It was a good job we'd finished

our bacon sandwiches because the only appetite we needed now was an appetite for danger.

"What did they say?" asked Harry, brushing breadcrumbs off his jumper and then pushing the frying pan to one side.

WORLD DEFENCE SUPER-DANGEROUS BRIEFING TIP:

Remember, if you are briefing your team on a mission that is super dangerous, always tell it to them straight.

I decided to tell it to them straight.

"If you think spybrows and hair-drying mammoths sound dangerous, then times that danger by a hundred," I whispered. "In fact, times it by a thousand, because it isn't just Valentino living in that house. No, there is something hairier, scarier, hungrier and more dangerous than anything an evil scientist has ever invented before . . ."

"What is it?" said Harry, preparing himself for the worst.

"Yes, what is it?" Colin shivered, preparing himself for worse than worst.

"It's the Hairy Horror from Hell." I shuddered.

"The Hairy Horror from WHAT?!"

"The Hairy Horror from HELL!"

"How big is it?" asked Harry.

"It's growing all the time," I told him. "The more haircuts Valentino does, the hairier it gets."

"How hairy is it?" asked Colin.

"Even its hairs have got hairs," I told him.

"How evil is it?" asked Colin.

"Evil with a capital E," I whispered.

"How hungry is it?"

"It hasn't eaten for six weeks."

"SIX WEEKS!" gasped Harry. "It's going to be starving!"

"Hungry enough to eat everyone in our whole town!" gasped Colin.

"Hungry enough to eat everyone

in the whole universe," I warned them. "Everyone except its one and only master of Evil and Hairiness himself . . . Valentino."

It was the most spine-tingling meeting we had ever had. Up until now our whole summer holiday had been full of missions we could easily handle. Now, suddenly, three end-of-holiday haircuts had led us to the hairiest, scariest mission of our lives.

If I'd had any doubts about whether Harry and Colin would be up to the job, my worries soon disappeared.

"Our mission today," I said, "is to

cycle to Valentino's house and save our homes, our school, our town and our universe from the biggest, hairiest, evillest and hungriest Hairy Horror the world has ever faced. It's going to be the riskiest thing we've ever done, and to be honest there is every chance that none of us will make it back alive – although I probably will because I'm a fully-trained world defence agent. So, Harry, so, Colin – are you ready to save the world? Are you ready to do battle with the Hairy Horror from Hell!?"

"BRING IT ON!" cheered Colin

and Harry, rubbing each other's heads for good luck and then rough-and-tumbling across the floor.

"SAVE YOUR ENERGY!" I told them. "If we're going to take on the Hairy Horror, we will need to be in tip-top shape – plus we need to arm ourselves like never before!"

"What weapons are we going to need?" asked Harry.

"I'm still deciding," I said, crawling back out of the tunnel. "I'll let you know as soon as I've had a good think."

Harry and Colin were totally up for a battle with a Hairy Horror and couldn't wait to get started.

"Don't forget to put the lid on the water butt!" I commanded. "And no overtaking me on your bikes!"

CHAPTER 20

As soon as we were within sight of Harry's house, I gave Harry and Colin the signal to slow down and then jumped off my bike.

While I was pedalling I had worked out what weapons we would need for our Hairy Horror mission. They weren't just any weapons, they were weapons specially designed to tackle anything that an evil hairdresser might throw at us.

All we had to do now was arm ourselves while our mums and dads weren't looking.

"OK, men," I said. "This is the specialist equipment we're going to need to fight the Hairy Horror. Listen to it, look for it and, if you can, get it:

hairdryers
curling tongs
hairbrushes
talcum powder
hairspray."

"I won't be able to get all of

those," said Colin. "My mum doesn't use hairspray."

"My mum doesn't curl her hair," said Harry, "so I won't be able to get any tongs."

"Just get what you can," I told them, "and make sure your parents don't see you while you're getting them."

Any other day of the week, weapon gathering could have been tricky, but Harry and Colin's parents always go food shopping on Saturday mornings, so no one would be in to stop them.

I knew Harry and Colin wouldn't let me down.

Things were going to be a bit riskier for me.

My mum and dad never go food shopping on a Saturday morning – they always have a lie-in till at least the afternoon. To get the weapons I needed, I was going to have to sneak into the house while they were still asleep and smuggle stuff out without them hearing or seeing me. If they woke up, I'd be rumbled!

Thank goodness they were still really tired from their mission the night before. In fact they were so tired, they were still wearing their daytime clothes!

Just like Harry and Colin, there were certain things that I wouldn't be able to get. My mum's hairspray was far too close to her bedside table for me to risk waking her, and the talcum powder in the bathroom had completely run out. Apart from that, though, I was pretty pleased with my haul.

When I met Harry and Colin at the bottom of my drive, I knew straight away that we were totally in business! Between us we had everything on my list. Thanks to our weapon-gathering skills, some things we had two of. Hairdryers we even had three of!

"Let's do this!" I said, cramming all our weapons into my mission rucksack and jumping back on my bike.

"It's time to teach Valentino and his Hairy Horror a lesson they won't forget!"

CHAPTER 21

At 11:02 hundred hours, we arrived
in Valentino's road.

WORLD DEFENCE DAYLIGHT-SURVEILLANCE TIP:

When approaching an evil
enemy's base in broad daylight,
use every available piece
of cover to hide behind.

The instant we were within sight of his front door, we laid our bikes down on the pavement on the other side of the road and took cover behind a parked car.

"Are you sure Valentino has gone to work?" whispered Harry, peeping over the car bonnet.

Valentino's house looked empty all right, but I knew from my shadow mission that a hideously hairy danger was lurking inside.

I gave a thumbs-up and then tugged him down by his sleeve.

"Are we going to take a look through the front window?" asked Harry.

"Too risky," I whispered. "The Hairy Horror could be hiding behind the curtains waiting for me to come back."

"What if it smells us?" asked Colin. "What if it hasn't just got a super-hairy body but super-sniffing hairy nostrils too?"

"You're right," I w h i s p e r e d , sucking my finger and then holding it up in the air. "If this mission is going to be successful, then we need to surprise the Hairy Horror, not the other way round."

My finger-sucking skills gave me all the information I needed.

"The wind is blowing towards the house," I whispered. "That means, if we approach Valentino's house from the front garden, the breeze behind us could blow our scent straight through the letter box and right up the Hairy Horror's super-sniffing hairy nostrils. If it smells us before we surprise it, it could have us for breakfast!"

"What are we going to do?" whispered Harry.

"I'll tell you what we're going to do." I smiled. "We're going to go in round the back!"

It was a brilliant change in

tactics. There was no way the Hairy Horror would be expecting us to come in through the back garden and no way it would be able to sniff us if we approached the house from downwind.

"If we go in round the back, the element of surprise will be totally ours!" I explained. "But before we go anywhere we need to activate our weapons!"

WORLD DEFENCE WEAPON-ACTIVATION TIP:

Leave it to an expert.

Luckily for Harry and Colin, I am an expert on activating weapons.

I'd had to use my skills to make mammoth-busting weapons in Dino Valley. Now I was going to need all the skills and know-how I had to create enough firepower to stop the Hairy Horror in its tracks!

As soon as I had emptied our rucksack, I set to work turning ordinary hairdressing equipment into awesome hair-busting weapons. Within five minutes we were armed to the hilt!

By 11:15 my work was done.

AGENT J GOES TO WORK!

Before

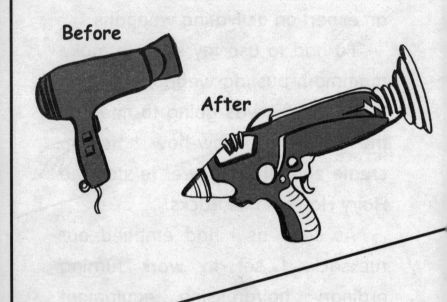

After

Before

After

Before   After

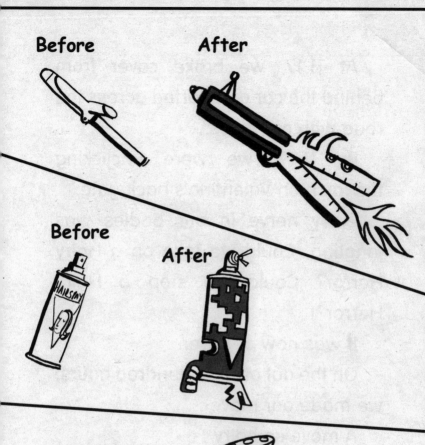

Before

After

Before

After

At 11:17, we broke cover from behind the car and darted across the road with our bikes.

By 11:19, we were unclicking the latch on Valentino's back gate.

Every nerve in our bodies was jangling. Could we take on a Hairy Horror? Could we stop a Hairy Horror?!

It was now or never.

On the dot of 11:20 hundred hours, we made our move . . .

A move so hairy . . .

A move so scary . . .

If you wet yourself easily . . .

Look away NOW!

GARDEN OF FEAR.

IT WAS DEATHLY QUIET WHEN THE THREE BRAVE AGENTS ENTERED THE BACK GARDEN OF THE EVIL ENEMY SCIENTIST.

PATIO OF PERIL!

TOWARDS THE EVIL
BUILDING THEY CRAWLED.

MOMENT OF TRUTH!

BRAVELY THEY RAISED THEIR EYES TO

THE WICKED WINDOW LEVEL . . .

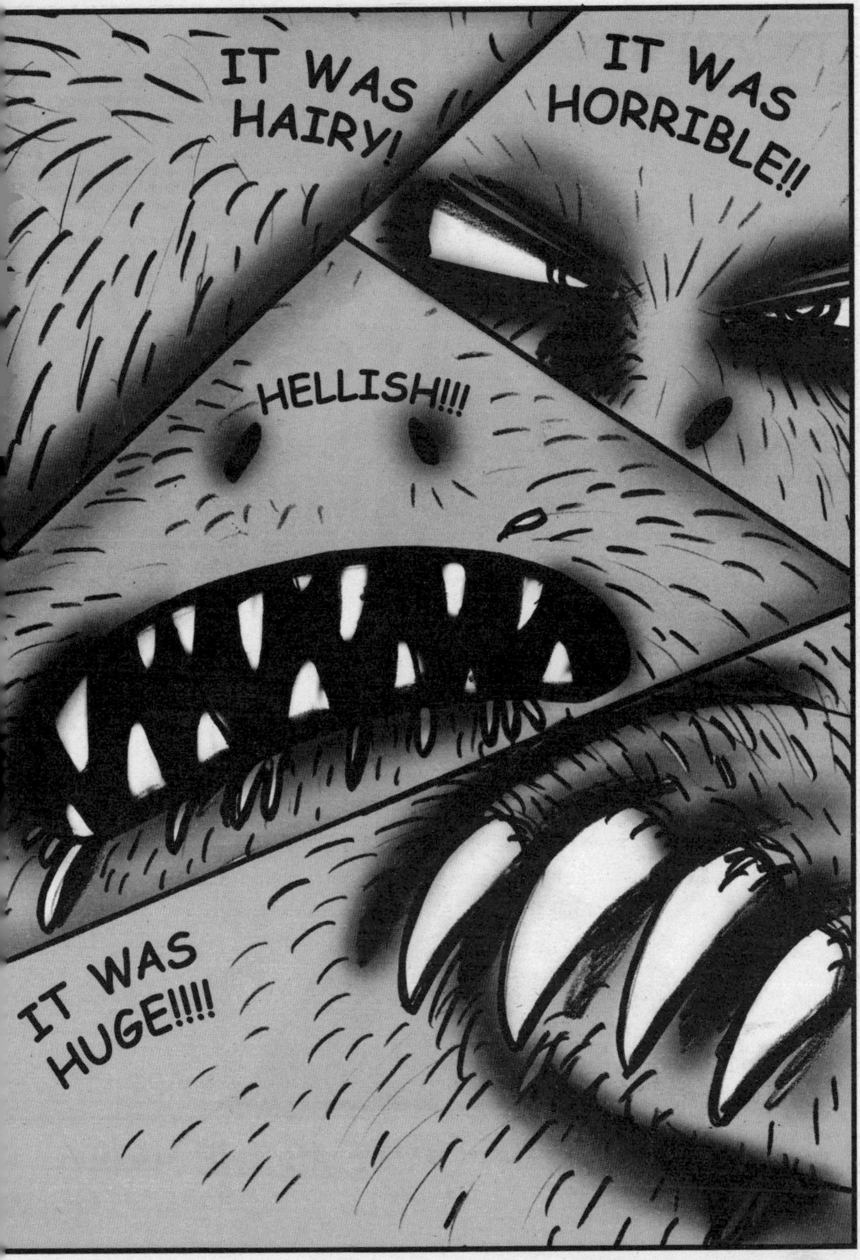
IT WAS HAIRY!
IT WAS HORRIBLE!!
HELLISH!!!
IT WAS HUGE!!!!

FROZEN WITH FEAR!

HARRY AND COLIN FROZE AS THE HAIRY HORROR ROSE.

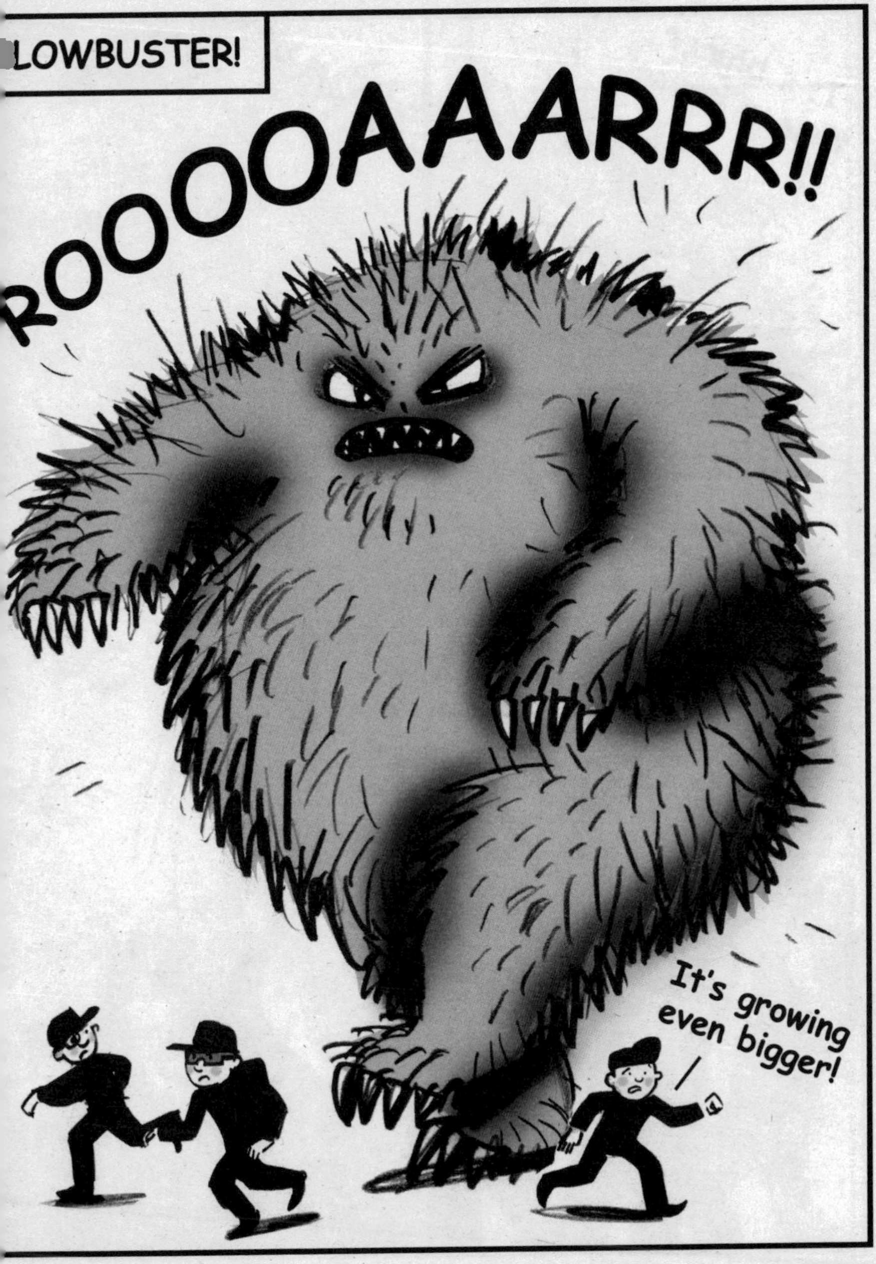
LOWBUSTER!
ROOOOAAAARRRR!!
It's growing even bigger!

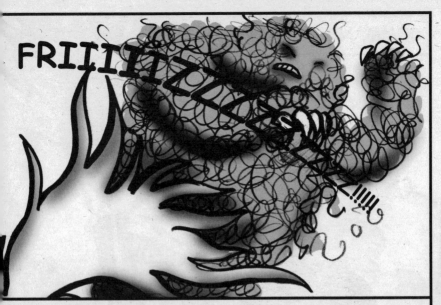

HARRY AND AGENT J UNLEASHED THE
AWESOME POWER OF THEIR COSMIC CURLERS.

COLIN LET RIP WITH A SMOKE CANISTER.

THE HAIRY HORROR ROARED AS ITS HAIR BEGAN TO CURL.

IT WAS TRUE. AS THE CLOUD OF SMOKE MELTED AWAY, SO DID THE HAIRY HORROR.

WHEN THE SMOKE VANISHED, ALL WAS REVEALED . . .

THE **HIDEOUSLY HUMUNGOUS HAIRY HORROR FROM HELL** HAD COMPLETELY SHRUNK . . .

TO THE SIZE OF A SMALL YAPPING DOG!

CHAPTER 22

We had done it! Against all the odds we had defeated the Hairy Horror and stopped Valentino completely in his tracks. The world was safe and we were victorious!

I would love to have seen Valentino's face when he got home on

Saturday evening and found that his humungously hideous Hairy Horror from Hell had been reduced to the size of a small dog!

Imagine how high his eyebrows would have gone then!

CHAPTER 23

When me, Colin and Harry went back to school after the holidays, it was like the world had never been at risk.

We weren't the only ones who had had their hair cut at Valentino's before going back to school, but we were the only ones who knew how close Valentino had come to using his evil haircuts to take over the world.

Colin and Harry reckon we should

have got medals for saving the universe, but as I've said before, medals aren't my style. Being a world defence agent isn't about that; it's about hard work, awesome defence skills and, most importantly, never giving up on a mission, however super-hairy things get.

Or super-tiring.

Take my mum and dad, for example. They are still so worn out from their last mission they haven't even noticed my new haircut!

I so, so want to be like them.

WORLD DEFENCE TIP:

Always carry a small pad and pen in case you need to make emergency notes. If you don't have a pad, make one out of something else.

WORLD DEFENCE TIP:

Beware of upside-down newspapers. People reading upside-down newspapers are only pretending to read their newspapers. They are definitely spies and have probably got their eyes on you!

WORLD DEFENCE TIP:

Beware of people reading foreign newspapers. If you see someone reading a foreign newspaper, they could be a foreign agent. If they are reading a foreign newspaper upside down, they are definitely a foreign agent.

WORLD DEFENCE TIP:

Beware of newspapers with eyeholes. If you see anyone reading a newspaper or magazine with eyeholes cut out, then they are using the eyeholes to spy on you. If you see someone reading an upside-down foreign newspaper with eyeholes, RUN!

WORLD DEFENCE SECURITY TIP:

If you need to contact World Defence HQ fast to ask them important questions, make sure your left earlobe has been fitted with a two-way communication device. An invisible chip will arouse no suspicion and can be activated at any time by one press of your earlobe.

WORLD DEFENCE DINOSAUR-APPROACH TIP:

Always camouflage your bikes before entering dinosaur territory. Otherwise they might get eaten.

WORLD DEFENCE
WEAPON-MAKING TIP:

Use things in the environment to craft awesome mission-winning weapons.

SURVIVAL TIP:

Use finger-sucking skills to check changes in wind speed and direction.

WORLD DEFENCE ESCAPE TIP:

If you're cornered by a hairdresser who isn't a real hairdresser, but he's asking you for real money, RUN!

WORLD DEFENCE TIP:

If you are being chased by the enemy in a helicopter, jump off your bike, cover yourself with camouflage and lie low.

WORLD DEFENCE CLOSE-QUARTER SURVEILLANCE TIP:

Always work out the position of the enemy inside a location before commencing your surveillance. Or you might find that he is the one watching you!

WORLD DEFENCE SPOTLIGHT·AVOIDANCE TIP:

If you are caught in a spotlight during a shadow mission, don't move a muscle.

WORLD DEFENCE MISSION PLAN A TIP:

Always have a Plan B.

WORLD DEFENCE DAYLIGHT SURVEILLANCE TIP:

When approaching an evil enemy's base in broad daylight, use every available piece of cover to hide behind.

Have you read this awesome Jack adventure?

Jack Beechwhistle is here to protect the world from alien
attacks, zombie sweet-shop owners and exploding conkers.
His missions are always dangerous and deadly, but
Jack's about to face his most challenging test yet:
the Attack of the Giant Slugs.

It's the Easter holidays. Daisy has been
given the school hamsters to look after,
plus FREE TICKETS TO CHOCOLATE LAND!

Daisy is SO ready for Chocolate Land.

TROUBLE IS, is Chocolate Land ready for Daisy?

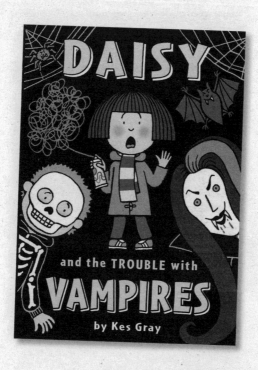

It's Halloween and Daisy is going trick-or-treating
for the very first time.
In the dark . . .
in the fog . . . .
with a VAMPIRE . . .
armed only with a torch and some silly string.

GULP!

Daisy loves surprises! Especially special
birthday surprises – like a trip to the ZOO!!!
Who'd have guessed a rhino could do so much
wee all in one go! Who'd have imagined
an elephant tooth was that heavy!

TROUBLE is, the biggest surprise
is yet to come.

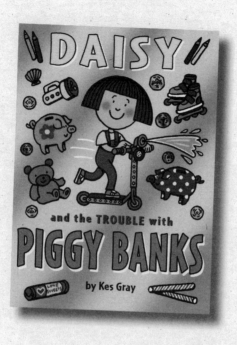

When Daisy's best friend Gabby gets the most
awesome, immense, water-squirting
micro-scooter Daisy's ever seen, Daisy
knows she's got to have one too!
Trouble is, they cost a LOT of money.

So Daisy and Gabby hatch a money-making
plan – what could possibly go wrong?